The Legend of
Dave the Villager 19

By Dave Villager

Third Print Edition (June 2021)

www.davethevillager.com
www.facebook.com/davevillager

Email me at: davevillagerauthor@gmail.com

BOOK NINETEEN:
The Frozen Ocean

CAST OF CHARACTERS

Dave
A villager looking for adventure. He's on a quest to find an end portal and slay the Ender Dragon.

Carl
A sarcastic creeper. Dave's best friend.

Spidroth
Herobrine's daughter. Finally got her real body back.

Big Billy
A baby zombie who got transformed into a big zombie.

Captain Nitwit
The captain of the HMS Nitwit. His eyes were replaced with spiders eyes. It's a long story...

LAST TIME

Dave and his friends survived Laboratory 303 and made their escape in a submarine. However, as they headed further and further west, the ocean around them grew cold and icy. Now their submarine has frozen up and is plunging towards the bottom of the ocean...

CHAPTER ONE

20,000 Blocks Under the Sea

"What are we going to do?!" screamed Captain Nitwit. "What are we going to do?"

The submarine was falling fast, sinking further and further into the dark, murky depths of the ocean.

"Eve," said Dave, "is there any chance you can get this thing working again?"

"Negative," said Eve, her hologram image flickering. "Soon I will... be unable... to even power myself. I hope you have... enjoyed this journey... with Laboratory 303 Submarines. We hope... to see you... again... soon."

Dave looked out of one of the windows. They were a fair way down from the surface, but they still had a long way to fall. Below them was only shadow, the bottom of the ocean too deep to see.

"Alright, we have no choice," Dave shouted. "We have to break free of the submarine and swim to the surface."

"Are you insane?" snapped Spidroth.

"Dave, my golem suit won't float," said Carl. "It'll just sink to the bottom."

"Then you'll have to leave it behind," said Dave. "I'm sorry everyone, but we have no choice. If we don't get out, we're going to sink to the bottom of the ocean."

"We'll never make it to the surface," said Carl, looking through a window. "We'll run out of air."

Dave took another look outside, searching desperately for a bubble column. Using bubble columns had been how he and Porkins had survived swimming underwater before, but Dave couldn't see any.

CLUNK!!!

Suddenly the submarine came to a sudden stop. Dave looked out of the window and could see nothing but darkness. They'd finally reached the ocean bed. He took another look up at the surface, but it was so far above them that he could barely see the sun. There was no way they'd survive swimming to the surface now.

"Well, it's too late now, anyway," said Dave. "It looks like we're trapped. Trapped at the bottom of the ocean."

"And just when I'd finally got my body back," said Spidroth, slumping down on one of the armchairs. "I blame you fools for this."

"Power... shutting... down," said Eve. Then her hologram flickered for a final time and she was gone. A moment later the redstone lamps inside the submarine all turned off, leaving Dave and his friends in total darkness.

Dave took out a torch from his bag and placed it on the ground, filling the dark room with a dim orange light. Then he took flint and steel from his bag and re-lit the netherrack fireplace.

The submarine was starting to get really cold, so they all gathered around the fire. Before long, even that wasn't enough, so they took blankets from the bed and wrapped them around their bodies. Big Billy was so big that he had to use four blankets.

"BRRR," said Big Billy.

"W-well?" said Carl, his teeth chattering. "N-now what?"

"I-I almost f-forgot," said Spidroth. "I h-have this."

She took out her long, double-handed iron sword and turned it on. The blade glowed red, giving off a huge amount of heat.

"I swear I've seen that sword before," said Carl, his teeth chattering slightly less as the glowing sword warmed up the room.

"It's similar to the sword Future Dave had," said Dave. "Although not exactly the same. I guess in Future Dave's timeline, the scientist who built that sword eventually went on to build weapons for Future Dave and the resistance."

"Future Dave? What are you babbling about?" said Spidroth. "We should be concentrating on how we're going to get out of here!"

Dave looked all around the submarine, racking his brain to find a solution to their problem, but he couldn't think of anything. There was a chest in the corner, but when he opened it all he found were seven splash potions of strength, some bone meal and an apple. He put all of it in his rucksack, then sat back down with his blanket.

"Well, at least that stupid glowing sword is keeping us warm," said Carl. "So we can starve to death rather than freezing to death."

"This blade must have incredible power to burn with such heat," said Spidroth, turning the sword around in her hands. "It is a fine weapon, to be sure."

"I wonder if it's hot enough to boil the ocean," said Carl sadly. "We could boil up all the water, then walk back to shore."

"Wait…" said Dave, "that's it!"

"Er, I was joking," said Carl. "I don't think the sword would actually be able to boil the entire ocean."

"No," said Dave, "but it might boil up enough water to create a bubble column! We can plunge the blade into the ocean floor to create a bubble column, and we can use the bubbles to give us enough air to swim to the surface!"

"What about my blade, fool?" said Spidroth. "It would be stuck at the bottom of the ocean."

"Um, yes," said Dave. "But at least we'd be alive."

"Pah," said Spidroth. "And you think this plan will work?"

"I do," said Dave. "I remember the weaponsmith in our village used to plunge the hot iron tools into water when he'd made them. The water used to bubble up like crazy."

"Yes, but wouldn't that be boiling water?" said Carl. "I don't want to get turned into a baked creep-tato."

"The water's so cold down here that it shouldn't be a problem," said Dave. "Plus, we'll be swimming far above the blade, just breathing in the air bubbles."

"Well," said Captain Nitwit, "it sounds like a top plan to me. The only trouble is, I can't swim."

Everyone looked at him.

"You're the captain of a ship but you can't swim?" said Dave in disbelief. "Weren't you ever worried about falling in the water?"

"Oh yes," said Captain Nitwit with a grin. "Frightfully worried."

"I will carry you, fool," said Spidroth. "Lady Spidroth is a master swimmer."

"Are you sure, Spidroth?" said Dave. "I'm assuming you haven't swum in thousands of years."

"You think I have forgotten how to swim?" snapped Spidroth.

"No, I was just, er, making sure," said Dave. "Does anyone know if Little Billy can swim?"

"*Big* Billy," said Spidroth.

"Right, Big Billy," said Dave. "Big Billy, can you swim?"

"BURR," said Big Billy, nodding his head.

"I'm gonna assume that's a yes," said Dave.

"I can't swim that well," said Carl. "I've only got small legs."

"I'll carry you," said Dave.

"I can't believe I'm gonna lose another set of golem armor," sighed Carl.

"BURR," said Big Billy, and he went over and picked up Carl's diamond armor by the arm, then threw it over his shoulder.

"That's very kind of you, Big B," said Carl, "but I can't ask you to do that."

"BURR, BURR, BURR!" said Big Billy, keeping hold of the armor.

"Right, well we ought to get a move on," said Dave. "Spidroth, can I have your sword?"

"Pah," said Spidroth, turning off the glowing blade and handing it hilt-first to Dave. Dave put it in his belt.

"Ok," said Dave, "here's what's going to happen. I'm going to use my pickaxe to break a hole in the side of submarine. The water's gonna come rushing in fast, and it's gonna be cold. I need to build a hole big enough for us all to get through, so I'm gonna keep destroying the blocks until I've made a hole three blocks tall by three blocks wide. Then I'm gonna swim out and you're all going to follow me. I'm going to plunge Spidroth's sword into the ocean floor to create the bubble column, then we're all going to swim to the surface, using the air from the bubble column to breathe. Has everyone got that?"

"What could possibly go wrong?" sighed Carl.

"Right, here goes," said Dave. "Carl, jump up on my shoulders. Spidroth, you're in charge of looking after Captain Nitwit."

"The fool will be safe with me," said Spidroth. "I will try my best to get him safely to the surface. But, to be honest, if he dies it will be no big loss."

"What?!" said Captain Nitwit. "I want to go with someone else!"

"Spidroth, bring Captain Nitwit safely to the surface or I'll find a way to get your mind transferred back into a chicken," said Dave. "That's a promise."

Spidroth frowned but didn't say anything. Captain Nitwit looked very worried.

Dave took out his diamond pickaxe and walked over to the iron-block wall of the submarine. Carl crawled up his back and got on his shoulders.

If I survive this, I really must learn about enchantments, thought Dave, looking at his pickaxe. He was sure that with an enchanted diamond pickaxe he would have been able to cut through the iron blocks even quicker.

Dave took a deep breath to compose himself, then hit one of the iron blocks with his pickaxe: *ching, ching, ching!*

WOOSH!!! Suddenly the iron block broke and freezing cold water started pouring into the submarine through the hole. Dave was almost swept back, but he just about managed to keep his footing.

"Everyone hold on!" Dave yelled. "I have to make the hole bigger!"

Dave hacked away at another block: *ching, ching, ching!* That one broke too, and water began pouring in at an even faster rate.

I've still got to break seven more blocks, thought Dave, started to panic. The water was already up to his waist, and it was rising fast.

"Hurry up, you cretin!" Spidroth yelled.

Dave broke the third block as fast as he could, then quickly broke the fourth. Then, suddenly, he lost his footing and went flying back across the other side of the room, swept up in the water.

"Waa!" Carl yelled, as he went flying off Dave's shoulders.

The current was so strong that all of them were being swept backwards now, pinned against the opposite wall as the water continued to pour in. Dave tried to stride forward towards the half-finished hole, but he wasn't strong enough to push through the current.

The water was rising high now, so high that it was almost at Dave's chin.

"You've killed us all, fool!" shouted Spidroth.

"Oh, be quiet, Spidroth!" said Dave, shouting to make his voice heard over the sound of the water rushing in. "Everyone, if you have a pickaxe, break a hole in the submarine! We need to get out of here!"

The water was almost at the ceiling now. Dave took a deep breath as the water rose above his head.

Finally, the submarine was completely full of water. Dave looked around at his friends. Captain Nitwit was panicking, Spidroth was trying to hack away at the iron wall with a diamond sword, Carl was just looking around desperately, and Big Billy was pounding away at the iron wall with his fists. Spidroth and Big Billy had managed to break a couple of blocks, but they were going too slowly.

Dave tried to use his diamond pickaxe to hack away at the wall, but it was taking too long. His pickaxe moved slower in the water, and he was beginning to feel woozy from the lack of oxygen.

Wait, thought Dave, *what am I doing? I should be using Spidroth's sword.*

In the panic of the water flooding in, Dave had nearly forgotten about Spidroth's glowing sword. He turned it on and the blade glowed red, the water around it instantly bubbling.

Dave took a huge gulp of bubbles, the air filling his lungs.

"Mmmph mmph!" he yelled to the others.

They all swam over and took some gulps of oxygen. Then Dave had an idea.

Maybe this sword can melt through iron, he thought. *It's worth a try...*

So Dave took the glowing, two-handed blade and carefully thrust it into the wall. The first iron block it touched instantly melted, then disappeared, so Dave moved on to the next block, then the next. Before long he'd done it: he'd opened up a hole big enough for them to swim through!

Dave grabbed Carl under his arm, motioned for the others to follow him, then he swam out into the ocean. The water was freezing cold, but he forced himself to kick his legs and swim down to the ocean bed. He plunged the glowing sword into the ocean bed, leaving it half embedded in the gravel.

As Dave had hoped, a column of bubbles began to rise up from the glowing sword. Dave had no idea how long the sword would be able to stay lit underwater, but it should give them enough time to get to the surface, he reckoned.

Dave looked around and saw that the others had all escaped the submarine too. Spidroth was holding Captain Nitwit and Big Billy was holding Carl's golem suit. Carl was still safely under Dave's arm.

Dave pointed upwards, indicating that they should start swimming to the surface.

They all began swimming up, occasionally stopping to take a lungful of air from the bubble column. The water was so cold that Dave found it hard to move his limbs, but somehow he managed. Before long he could see the dim light of the sun above them.

We're nearly there, Dave thought happily. Once again they'd survived certain doom.

They were nearly at the surface now. The top of the water looked a bit misty, but Dave assumed that it must just be a cloudy day. He kicked his legs, looking forward to getting a big lung-full of air, but then *DONK*, he hit his head on something solid. Dave put his hand up and touched the solid thing above him. It was freezing cold.

Oh no, he thought. *The sea's frozen over! We're below ice!*

He looked around saw Spidroth, Captain Nitwit and Big Billy were starting to panic too, all of them realizing that there was no way to reach the surface. Dave turned to get another gulp of air from the bubble column, but then saw, to his horror, that there were no more bubbles. He looked down and could no longer see the distant glow of Spidroth's sword on the ocean bed.

The sword must have finally run out of power, thought Dave. *We're trapped and we've got no oxygen!*

Then he heard a deep banging sound: *DOOM DOOM DOOM!!!* Dave looked over and saw Big Billy banging on the ice. For a moment it looked like it wasn't going to break, then *CRACK*—he broke through, sunlight shining through the hole in the ice sheet.

Big Billy pulled himself up through the hole along with Carl's diamond golem armor, then he reached a hand back into the water and helped Spidroth and Captain Nitwit up too.

Dave swam over towards the hole, Carl still safely tucked under his arm. Big Billy plunged his big arm back down through the hole and Dave reached out his own hand to grab it...

... but then something grabbed his leg.

Dave looked down and saw a swarm of drowned below him, their pale blue eyes glowing in the darkness. They grabbed at his legs with their moldy fingers and began to pull him down with them. Dave screamed, the last of the oxygen leaving his lungs. He tried to kick his legs to swim upwards, but the drowned were too strong. He reached for his sword with his one free hand, but his fingers were too numb from the cold, and he fumbled it. The sword fell from his grip, disappearing into the depths of the ocean.

Well, if I'm going down, I'm not going to take Carl with me, thought Dave. He took Carl from under his arm and pushed him upwards. Carl turned around in the water to look back at him, but Dave motioned for him to flee.

Go on, Dave thought. *Get out of here, Carl! Save yourself!*

Suddenly a huge shape plunged into the ocean from the hole in the ice: It was Big Billy! The huge zombie swam down to Dave and Carl then went to town on the drowned: pulling them off Dave and smacking them with his huge fists.

"BURR!!!" Big Billy yelled, his voice so loud they could hear it through the water.

Free from the drowned, Dave swam up and grabbed Carl under his arm. He turned to check on Big Billy, but saw that the zombie was being overwhelmed by the drowned. They had grabbed his arms, his legs and his head and were pulling him under.

"BURR!!!!" yelled Big Billy.

Dave was so dizzy from a lack of oxygen that it was all that he could do not to pass out, but he had to save Big Billy. He reached for his sword, but then realized that he'd lost it.

Dave and Carl looked on helplessly as Big Billy was dragged deeper into the water by the drowned. The huge zombie was doing his best to fight them off, but there were simply too many of them.

"BURR!!!" Big Billy bellowed one final time, and then he was gone: disappearing into the dark depths of the ocean, dragged under by the drowned.

CHAPTER TWO
Packed Ice

Dave pulled himself and Carl out of the hole, then lay panting on the ice, trying to get his breath back.

"Where's Big Billy?" he heard Spidroth ask.

"He's... gone," said Dave, barely able to get the words out. "He's gone."

"Oh no," said Spidroth. And for the first time, Dave thought he detected something like sorrow in her voice.

"Where's he gone?" asked Captain Nitwit.

"He's gone as in... dead," said Dave.

"Oh," said Captain Nitwit, his face falling. "Oh dear. The poor little lad."

"He went out like a hero," said Carl. "He saved our lives."

Dave was surprised to see that even Carl was a bit tearful. The creeper was unusually quiet as he crawled back into his diamond golem armor.

Goodbye Little Billy, thought Dave. He'd grown oddly fond of the baby zombie during their brief time together. He was going to miss him.

Dave suddenly realized how cold he was. His clothes were soaking with freezing water and he was laying on a cold sheet of ice.

"W-we need to build some s-s-shelter and a f-fire," said Dave, pushing himself to his feet. His teeth were chattering from the cold.

For the first time, Dave got a proper look at their surroundings. They were standing in the middle of a vast expanse of endless ice. Most of the water around them was covered by sheets of blue ice, with a few pools of water scattered about. The water inside the pools was so dark that it almost looked purple. Huge iceberg hills rose up around them, made from a mixture of blue and white ice.

It was so cold that Dave could see the breath in front of his face. His fingers were so numb that he could barely move them, but he forced himself to open the zip of his rucksack and pull out a block of netherrack, slamming it onto the ice to make it full-size. Next he fumbled in his bag and pulled out some flint and steel, scraping it across the netherrack.

The netherrack block lit up, creating an instant fire. Dave held out his hands, getting as close to the fire as he dared. The heat felt amazing, and he could instantly feel his fingers getting less numb. Captain Nitwit and Carl walked over to join him, but Spidroth was looking at them as if they were all idiots.

"Y-y-you fools," she shivered, "b-building a f-f-fire on ice is n-not a v-- very clever ide—"

Suddenly the ground disappeared beneath Dave's feet and he plunged into the cold water. He kicked his legs and swam to the surface, coughing and spluttering. Carl and Captain Nitwit were both in the water too, inside a small pool that had formed around the netherrack block, which had now gone out. Thankfully Carl had managed to grab onto the side of the ice as he fell, or he and his diamond armor would have sunk to the bottom of the ocean.

"F-f-fire melts ice," said Spidroth, looking down at them from the side of the pool.

"H-h-help us out of h-h-here and s-stop lecturing us!" said Dave.

Carl pulled himself out of the ice using his huge golem arms, then Spidroth pulled Captain Nitwit and Dave out. Dave was even colder and wetter than before now. If they couldn't build a fire, what were they going to do?

"W-w-we n-n-need to build it on p-p-p-packed ice," said Spidroth. "C-c-come on."

She motioned for them to follow her. Dave and the others trudged across the ice behind Spidroth as she walked over towards one of the iceberg hills. Dave noticed that the iceberg was made of a slightly darker blue ice than the blue ice underneath their feet.

"G-g-give me the netherrack and the f-f-f-flint," said Spidroth, once they reached the bottom of the hill, holding out her hand.

Dave did as she asked. Spidroth placed the netherrack block on top of a block of dark-blue ice, then lit it. This time, the ice didn't melt. They all stood next to the fire, letting it warm them up.

"Packed ice doesn't melt," said Spidroth. "Don't you fools know anything?"

Once his hands were a bit less numb, Dave took out some wood from his bag and built them a small house around the flaming netherrack block, making sure to make the floor out of cobblestone so that the fire wouldn't spread. Finally they had a nice cozy house in the middle of the icy wasteland, and they sat down to relax around the fire.

"Does anyone want to say a few words about Little Billy?" asked Dave, as they tucked into some baked potatoes that Carl had cooked for them.

"Big Billy," Spidroth corrected him.

"I'll do it," said Carl. "Little Billy, Big Billy, whatever you want to call him, was one of the coolest little dudes I ever met. He wasn't the best chicken jockey, and he wasn't much of a talker, but he always defended his friends. Here's to the best baby zombie in the world, Little Billy."

"Little Billy," repeated Dave, Captain Nitwit and Spidroth.

Carl took a bite out of his baked potato.

"So," he said. "What now? We have no boat, we've lost a team member and we're in the middle of endless ice at the end of the world. What are we going to do?"

"We're going to do what we always do," said Dave. "We're going to throw an eye of ender up and see where it takes us."

CHAPTER THREE
The Skull

After a good night's sleep, Dave and the others left the house. Dave had made thick leather coats for him, Spidroth and Captain Nitwit, so that they wouldn't freeze, but Carl said his diamond golem suit was warm enough.

Dave took an ender eye out of his rucksack and threw it up into the air. It flew off into the distance, telling them which way they should travel.

"We can keep walking across the ice until we either hit land or the open ocean," said Dave.

"And what happens if the ice ends and we do end up at the ocean?" asked Spidroth. "We don't have a ship."

"We'll have to build ourselves boats," said Dave. "I don't like the idea of crossing the ocean on little wooden rowboats, but we may have no choice. It's either that or swim."

So they started walking. The going was slow, as they had to be careful not to lose their footing on the ice and slip over. The scenery around them was constant: an unending expanse of ice sheets, water pools and hills. Sometimes they could see the occasional polar bear in the distance, but thankfully the bears kept away from them. Once Dave looked down and was shocked to see a polar bear swimming in the water below the ice they were standing on. The bear swam up to a school of fish and grabbed one, before swimming away with it.

"Oh crumbs!" said Captain Nitwit, looking down at the bear. "I hope none of those bears come near us. I have a terrible fear of polar bears."

"I think everyone has a fear of polar bears," said Carl. "I mean, it would be dumb *not* to be afraid of polar bears."

"You don't understand," said Captain Nitwit, starting to panic, "I'm a proper bearophobic. I have bearophobia."

"Is that a real thing?" asked Dave.

"Probably," said Captain Nitwit.

By midday, Dave actually had to take his leather coat off because the sun was so strong. There were no clouds in the sky and the light was reflecting off the shiny surface of the ice. Dave was keen to not use up their food rations too quickly, so he built fishing rods for the four of them, and they went up to one of the holes in the ice and fished for their lunch. They each managed to catch a cod, so Dave put a smoker down and cooked the fish for them.

After they'd eaten, they set off again across the ice. They'd been walking for about an hour when Dave saw something strange up ahead. One of the icebergs in the distance seemed to be a strange shape: it looked a bit like a skull.

"Carl," said Dave, "can you see that iceberg over there—"

"That one that looks like a skull?" said Carl. "Yeah, I see it. Pretty weird."

Before long they were walking past the iceberg. Most of the iceberg had been carved to resemble a giant skull, with white ice for the head and blue ice for the eyes.

"I wonder how long that's been there," said Spidroth. "It could be thousands of years or it could have been carved last week. It's impossible to know with ice."

"And who carved it?" said Captain Nitwit. "It doesn't look like the work of polar bears."

Dave hoped that whoever had carved the skull was long gone. He felt an intense feeling of dread as they walked past it, as if the skull's blue eyes were staring into his very soul.

By late afternoon they had walked so far that their feet had begun to hurt, so they had another rest, sitting on the slopes of an iceberg hill.

"Maybe we should rest until morning," said Captain Nitwit.

"I think we should keep going until the sun goes down," said Dave. "We don't want to stay on this ice any longer than we have to. Plus, I want to put as much distance between us and that giant skull as possible."

So they kept walking. About an hour later they were coming around the side of a hill when they saw something unexpected up ahead: shipwrecks. There were at least ten of them, all half-frozen in the ice or stuck to the side of the icebergs.

"Ships!" said Carl excitedly. "Maybe we'll be able to use one!"

"Fool!" snapped Spidroth. "Those are merely shipwrecks. You'd have more luck sailing a cluckshroom."

"Captain Nitwit," said Dave, "I know you said you didn't know how to build a ship, but do you think it's possible we can use these bits of ships to make a whole one?"

"Maybe," said Captain Nitwit.

"Of course we can!" said Carl. "We've got all the bits of ship we need, and they all look like they're the same design of ship. We can melt the ice to get the ships free, then fit all the bits we need together. We'll definitely be able to do it."

The sun was starting to go down, the orange light glistening off the ice.

"Let's get some rest now and make a start on it tomorrow," said Dave. "I think Carl's right—this could really work!"

Dave built them another house on some nearby packed ice, then they lit a fire and settled into their beds.

As he snuggled up nice and warm under his covers, Dave was struck by how odd it was that he was in a small wooden house on the middle of an ice sheet, with the ocean below him and icebergs all around. From the inside, the cozy wooden house looked like it could have just been a normal wooden house in any village.

Dave was just starting to drift off to sleep when he heard something rattling the door.

Oh no, please don't be another Laboratory 303 monster, he thought, but then he realized he was being stupid—they were miles away from Lab 303 now.

Everyone else was asleep, so Dave cautiously got out of bed, walked over to the oak door and had a sneaky look through the window.

Oh no, he thought, quickly darting backwards away from the door. *Oh no, oh no, oh no!*

The thing nuzzling at their door was a polar bear: a full-sized, adult polar bear. And the worst thing was, the bear wasn't alone. All around their house were endless polar bears—maybe hundreds of them.

Dave ducked down next to his bed, to avoid the polar bears seeing him through any of the windows.

The bashing at the door became more intense. The polar bear was *really* trying to get in. Dave could hear the other polar bears around the house as well, testing the strength of the wooden walls with their paws, trying to see if they could break them.

"What's going on?" Carl mumbled from his bed. "What's all that banging?"

"Sssh!!!" said Dave, putting a finger to his lips. "There are polar bears outside."

Spidroth was awake now too.

"Did you say polar bears?" she whispered.

"What's everyone talking about?" muttered Captain Nitwit. "Is it morning already? I'm tired."

"There are polar bears outside," whispered Dave.

"What?" said Captain Nitwit sleepily. "Roller hairs?"

"No," whispered Dave. "Polar bears."

"Molar fairs?"

"No," said Dave. "Polar... bears!!!"

"Oh," said Captain Nitwit, sitting up and rubbing the sleep from his eyes. "Polar bears."

Suddenly the color drained from Captain Nitwit's face.

And then he screamed.

CHAPTER FOUR

Bears

"ARRRGGGHHHHH!!!!!!"

As soon as Captain Nitwit screamed, the bears went crazy, pounding at the wooden house and roaring angrily, trying to break their way in.

Some of the bears broke through the glass of the windows, sticking their heads through and trying to get at Dave and the others.

"Oh gosh, oh gosh, oh gosh!" whimpered Captain Nitwit, hiding under his bed covers. "This is a nightmare! This is a nightmare!"

"Everyone stay away from the walls!" yelled Dave. "And get your weapons ready. That includes you, Nitwit!"

Dave and Spidroth quickly put on their armor, and Carl crawled into his diamond golem suit.

"Come on, Nitwit, armor up!" said Spidroth, dragging Captain Nitwit out of bed.

Reluctantly, Captain Nitwit put on his diamond armor.

"Right," said Dave, "let's try to drive them away with arrows."

He had three wooden bows in his rucksack, so he gave one to Spidroth, one to Captain Nitwit and kept one for himself.

"Fire as many arrows at them as you can," said Dave, "but if they break in you may need to switch to swords."

"Do not try to instruct me in the ways of battle, cretin!" snapped Spidroth. "I was fighting monsters before you were born!"

"Yes, we all know you're old, stop going on about it," said Carl.

"They're not going to break in, are they?" whimpered Captain Nitwit. "Please say they're not going to break in!"

"Not if I can help it," said Dave.

22

The bears had managed to break some of the wooden blocks of the walls in places, and were becoming more and more aggressive as they tried to break in. Dave took aim with his bow and fired an arrow at the snout of a bear that had put its head through a window.

"ROOAR!!" the bear yelled in pain, pulling its head out from the window. Spidroth and Captain Nitwit fired arrows too, hitting other bears.

"It's working!" said Dave. "Keep it up!"

Their wooden house was full of holes now, with bear snouts and paws poking through all of them, so it wasn't hard to find targets to hit. Dave fired arrow after arrow as fast as he could. The bears that were hit with arrows ran off in pain, but then other bears would take their place, all of them angry and looking for a meal.

"I hope you're ready, Carl," said Dave, firing another arrow. "I think the bears are going to be breaking in soon."

"Don't worry about me, I'm ready," said Carl. "These bears are gonna get a clobbering."

Suddenly there was an explosion of wood behind them, and Dave turned to see that the bears had broken a big hole in one of the walls.

"ROOOAAR!!!!"

A bear pushed its way through the hole, into the house, but Carl was ready for it. *POW!* He punched the bear right in the nose. The bear quickly backed out of the hole, but the other bears were busy destroying the blocks around the hole, making it wider. As Dave, Spidroth and Captain Nitwit continued to shoot arrows at the bears on one side of the room, Carl fought off polar bears pouring through the big hole on the other side. Dave was too busy firing arrows to look back, but he could see Carl wrestling and punching the bears out of the corner of his eye. All around them they could hear the sound of bears roaring.

"If I get out of this alive, I'm going to have nightmares for the rest of my life," whimpered Captain Nitwit.

"Just keep fighting," said Dave. "We can win this."

Dave could see the sun starting to rise on the horizon through the holes in the wooden house.

How long have we been fighting? he wondered. His fingers were hurting from firing his bow, but he knew that he had to keep going.

Dave had put all the arrows he had on the floor next to him, Captain Nitwit and Spidroth, so they could easily reach for another handful when they needed more. But this time when Dave reached down to grab more arrows... there were none left.

"We're out of arrows!" said Captain Nitwit, looking down at the empty space on the floor. "We're going to die! I'm going to die and I never even got to see a mooshroom!"

"Swords out," said Dave.

Spidroth and Captain Nitwit fired the rest of their arrows at the bears, then they all pulled out their swords.

"Have at thee, bears!" yelled Spidroth, hitting a bear on the snout with her sword.

Dave joined her, whacking the bears sticking their heads through the holes with his sword.

"Come on," Dave said to Captain Nitwit, who was cowering in the middle of the room, "we need your help!"

"I'm not getting close to the bears!" whimpered Captain Nitwit.

"FOOL, YOU WILL DO AS YOU'RE TOLD!" yelled Spidroth. "NOW FIGHT!"

"Um, ok then," said Captain Nitwit, and he cautiously got as near to the wall as he dared, then started whacking the bears with his sword.

Dave was pleased to see that even though Captain Nitwit was afraid, he was doing his best to fight the bears.

"Back, you bears!" said Captain Nitwit, giving a bear a gentle whack on the head with his sword.

"Wait," said Dave, moving away from the wall and pulling out his rucksack. "I forgot, I found these on the submarine."

He pulled out two of the splash potions of strength.

"Here," said Dave, chucking one of the potions to Spidroth. "Drink this."

"Fool!" said Spidroth. "This is a splash potion, not a drinking potion!"

"Then splash it on yourself!" said Dave.

Spidroth smashed the bottle against the side of her neck. The glass shattered and the dark red potion was absorbed into her skin.

"I do feel a bit stronger," she admitted. "Now to teach these bears not to mess with Spidrothbrine!"

And she charged with her sword, hitting the bears trying to get through the wall.

"Head's up, Nitwit," said Dave, and he threw a potion at Captain Nitwit's back, where it shattered onto his clothes.

"Thanks Dave," said Captain Nitwit, "that should keep me going for a bit longer!"

"Come on Dave, share the love," said Carl. So Dave took another bottle and threw it at the creeper's head.

"Oh yeah," said Carl, clenching his diamond fists, "that's more like it!"

And he ran back into the battle, biffing the polar bears who were trying to break into the house.

Finally Dave took a bottle and smashed it gently against the side of his face. The liquid absorbed into his skin and he felt an intense strength flow through him. He gripped his sword and charged back into the battle.

The potion of strength gave them all the boost they needed to keep going a bit longer, but it wasn't long before it wore off, and they were all starting to get exhausted.

The sun was fully up now, but the bears kept coming. Dave's sword hand was aching, and he was feeling so sleepy and tired, but he knew that if he stopped they would all get eaten.

"I... don't think... I can go on much longer," said Captain Nitwit wearily.

"You don't have a choice, fool!" snapped Spidroth.

Two of the walls of the house had completely broken now, so Carl was having to fight off the bears from two angles, but he was still doing a good job, punching and wrestling the bears as best he could.

Suddenly Dave heard another sound over all the roaring and smashing: the sound of arrows. Someone outside the house was firing arrows at the bears. The bears roared in pain and frustration as they were hit by a hail of arrows raining down from the sky. Some of the bears were slain and went *POOF*, and the others all ran off.

"We're saved!" said Captain Nitwit happily. "Someone saved us!"

The house was nothing but a ruin now, so Dave didn't even need to look through a window to see who had fired the arrows. Standing on the iceberg hills all around them were hundreds of skeletons in gray rags holding bows.

No, thought Dave. *Not skeletons... strays.*

CHAPTER FIVE
Strays

"What do we do?" Carl asked.

"I guess we don't have much of a choice," said Dave. "We can't fight them, so hopefully they're friendly. Let's go and speak to them."

Dave walked out from the ruins of the house onto the ice, followed by the others.

"Hello!" he shouted to the strays. "Thank you for saving us from the bears!"

There were hundreds of strays surrounding them. Their bones and rags were so blue and gray that if Dave hadn't known that they were there they could have easily remained hidden amongst the barren, icy landscape.

Some of the strays were riding on skeleton horses. They had capes, and looked like they were in charge, so Dave walked closer to them.

"We are grateful for your help," he said to the strays on horses, "and we can offer you gifts to say thank you. We have gold, diamonds, whatever you desire."

Can they even understand what I'm saying? Dave wondered, as the strays looked blankly back at him with their dead gray eyes.

Then one of the strays on horseback turned to one of the other strays and said something in a voice that sounded like the cracking of ice. It seemed to be talking in some strange language, and Dave couldn't understand a word of it.

The other stray laughed, then all the strays on horseback began to laugh. To Dave it sounded like cruel, mocking laughter.

"Maybe one of them just told a funny joke," Carl whispered.

The strays on horseback stopped laughing, then one of them trotted forward towards Dave and the others.

"You... speak... villager... language?" croaked the stray.

"Er, yes," said Dave.

"You... follow... us."

"Actually, we kind of have our own thing going on," said Carl. "And we're in a bit of a rush."

"Is... not... request," croaked the stray. It sounded like every word he spoke was hurting his throat. "You... come... with... us... or... we... slay... you."

"Right," said Dave. "In that case, I guess we don't have much of a choice."

"No... choice," croaked the stray. "We... take... you... to... Queen. She... decide... what... do... with... you."

"Well, at least their leader is a woman," said Spidroth. "That's what I like to see. Maybe I can speak to her woman to woman and sort this mess out. When I was a Queen, I was always praised for my diplomatic prowess."

"Red... woman... be... quiet," croaked the stray.

Carl laughed.

"Maybe these strays aren't so bad after all," he chuckled.

"Pah," said Spidroth.

So Dave and his friends reluctantly followed the strays across the ice. The strays on horseback rode on ahead, and the other strays surrounded Dave, Carl, Spidroth and Captain Nitwit, making sure that they couldn't escape.

"Could we at least stop for a spot of breakfast?" Captain Nitwit asked. "We didn't get much sleep last night, thanks to those bears."

But the strays ignored him.

"What are we going to do?" Carl whispered to Dave. "What if this queen of theirs wants to feed us to the polar bears or whatever?"

"We'll just have to keep our wits about us," said Dave. "I can't see any way of escaping yet, but we might get a chance later."

After a couple of hours walking across the ice under the harsh glare of the sunlight, they came across another huge skull carved into the side of an iceberg. Dave saw that in the distance there were other skulls carved into icebergs as well, and he even saw a statue of a gigantic stray made completely from ice.

"This must be a stray kingdom," said Spidroth. "I always thought that strays were no more than mindless savages."

"Maybe some of them are," said Carl. "I've met plenty of skeletons in my time. Some were intelligent and could speak, some were as thick as a bedrock block. I guess strays are the same."

"Look at that up ahead," said Captain Nitwit, pointing. "It looks like some sort of castle."

Dave looked at where Captain Nitwit was pointing. Sure enough, in the distance there was a huge castle with towers like spikes. It looked like it had been carved out of an iceberg.

"It looks like that's where they're taking us," said Carl.

As they got nearer to the castle they saw other buildings around them, all carved out of the icy hills. There were more statues as well, some of strays, some of polar bears, and even one that looked a bit like Steve.

"Even here I can't get away from Steve," sighed Dave.

"It could be Herobrine," said Carl, looking up at the statue. "Or even a drowned or a zombie. It's hard to tell when the only colors they have to use are blue and white. These strays need to get themselves some dyed wool or some colored concrete."

As they got nearer to the castle they saw some strays fishing with rods in pools of dark purple water. When they caught a fish they would put it in a chest, then dip their rod back in to catch another one.

Do strays even eat? wondered Dave. He'd always assumed that undead creatures like strays and skeletons didn't need food. Although he knew that zombies ate, so maybe strays were the same.

Finally they reached the huge castle. Its huge spiked towers cast a shadow over them as they walked up to it, and the entrance was carved in the shape of a skull with its mouth open.

"What a lovely place," said Carl.

The normal strays stood to one side, and the strays on horseback trotted up to Dave, Carl, Spidroth and Captain Nitwit.

"We... take... you... to... see... Queen... now," croaked one of the strays on horseback. Dave assumed it must be the same one who'd spoken to them before, but it was hard to tell as all the strays looked the same."

"Er, great," said Dave.

The strays on horseback surrounded Dave and his friends, then led them inside the castle.

This does not look good, thought Dave, looking up at the giant carved skull as they walked into its mouth. *This does not look good at all...*

CHAPTER SIX
The Queen

The inside of the castle was a twisted maze of narrow packed-ice corridors and steep staircases. It was dark too, with no torches or fires, lit only by the light coming in from the occasional window. As they reached the first set of ice stairs, the strays in capes dismounted their horses, and continued on foot.

Dave had to walk carefully to avoid falling over on the icy stairs. The strays led them up staircase after staircase, until finally they reached a huge throne room with a tall ceiling and big windows that overlooked the icy plains below. Dave was surprised to see that unlike the rest of the castle, which was cold and made from ice, the throne room was quite cozy. It had wooden walls, a plush blue carpet, glass in the windows and a roaring fire in the middle of a cobblestone fireplace. On a wooden throne in the middle of the room sat an old woman villager. She was either fast asleep or dead, Dave couldn't tell which.

"What's going on?" Carl whispered to Dave. "Is that their queen?"

The strays in capes each took a step forward and knelt in front of throne. One of them began talking to the old woman in the strange language that sounded like cracking ice. The old woman woke up, looking very confused.

"Oh hello, dears," she said, looking at the strays. "How are you young lads doing? Would you like a cup of milk? They say it's good for bones, so you lot should probably drink a lot of it."

She chuckled at her own joke.

"We... have... prisoners," said one of the strays.

"Ooh, so you do," said the old woman, noticing Dave and the others. "Come over here, dears. I don't bite."

Dave and his friends cautiously walked over, the strays in capes giving them evil stares.

"Oh, off with you," the old woman said to the strays, waving a hand. "You're scaring our guests. I may be an old woman, but I can look after myself, thank you very much. Go on, shoo!"

The strays gave Dave and the others threatening looks, then reluctantly left the room, closing the wooden doors behind them.

"I am sorry about them," said the old woman, giving Dave a smile. "They mean well, but they can be a bit unfriendly sometimes."

"What's going on here?" asked Spidroth. "Are those monsters holding you captive?"

"Oh goodness no, pet," chuckled the old lady. "No, I'm their queen. They wouldn't hurt a hair on my head."

"Right," said Carl, giving the old lady a funny look. "If you don't mind me asking, how did a villager end up being the queen of a bunch of strays? Are you some sort of witch?"

The old woman chuckled again.

"No, I'm not a witch," she said. "Just an ordinary old woman."

The old woman reached into a pocket and pulled out a pair of spectacles, putting them on and then staring at Dave and his friends.

"I must say, you are a funny-looking bunch," she said. "What are you, some sort of robot creeper?"

"Actually I'm a creeper wearing the body of a diamond golem," said Carl.

"Oh," said the old woman. "That's certainly something you don't see every day. And you, young lady, why's your skin so red?"

"*Young lady?*" said Spidroth angrily. "Woman, I was thousands of years old before you were born. You are but a child to me!"

"If you say so," said the old woman with a friendly smile. "I didn't wish to offend. I'm Doris by the way."

"Pleased to meet you Doris," said Dave. "I'm Dave."

"Carl," said Carl.

"Nitwit," said Captain Nitwit.

"The Lady Spidrothbrine, Queen of the Spiders," said Spidroth. "But you may call me Spidroth."

"So how did you come to be the queen of these strays?" Dave asked Doris.

"Yes, I admit it is a bit of a strange situation," said Doris, smiling. "I bet when they told you that you were going to meet their queen, you didn't expect to see someone like me!"

"We certainly didn't," said Captain Nitwit. "I was expecting some sort of ice monster or a giant stray with three heads or something."

"Goodness," said Doris, staring at Captain Nitwit through her spectacles, "have you got spider eyes? How fun!"

"Yes, they are rather nifty," grinned Captain Nitwit.

"I'm sorry," said Doris, turning back to Dave, "I keep getting distracted. You were asking how I came to be here, and I was about to tell you. Well, it all began quite a few years ago, when I was a child. My family and I were sailing across the ocean, in search of a new home, when suddenly our ship was struck by a storm. We went off course and crashed into an iceberg.

"I was the only one who survived. I was freezing and alone and I thought I wasn't going to make it, when the strays found me. They were going to kill me, but I managed to make a deal with them. I was allowed to live with them, and eventually learned to be one of them. I got quite nifty with a bow and arrow—although my fingers are far too old and frail to use one now!

"I taught the strays to speak my language and they taught me theirs. At least, I can understand it. I think it's impossible for villagers to actually speak it. Anyway, the strays grew to respect me so much that when their old king was slain by a polar bear, they put me in charge. That must have been thirty years or so ago, and I've been their queen ever since."

"What kind of queen are you?" asked Spidroth. "Are you ready to smite down those who are disloyal to you? That's how I ruled, and it always served me well."

"Oh dear me, no," giggled Doris. "I'm a nice queen. Or at least I hope so!"

"And are you sure you don't want rescuing?" asked Dave. "I don't know how yet, but we could get you out of here and bring you back to the mainland."

"Oh no," smiled Doris. "Thank you, but the strays are my people now. I couldn't imagine living anywhere else. I've got a lovely cozy room here and they look after me well. I mean, I do get a bit fed up of eating fish for every meal, but nowhere's perfect!"

"Well, as long as you're sure," said Dave. "In that case, would you mind asking the strays to let us leave? We want to be on our way, and were thinking of fixing up some of the shipwrecks to create a working ship of our own."

Doris chuckled.

"Oh no, I'm sorry dears, I can't let you leave," she said. "We don't get many visitors here, just the occasional crew of lost villagers or pillagers who've crashed into the ice. So when we do get some visitors, we sacrifice them."

"I'm sorry, what?" said Carl.

"We sacrifice them," repeated Doris, still smiling kindly. "The strays are fairly intelligent creatures, but they do have some strange beliefs. There's a big polar bear on the island who they believe is a god, so when we get strangers washing up on our shores, we sacrifice them to the bear. It's a bit rude, I know, but it keeps the strays happy."

"W-wait," said Captain Nitwit, "I don't understand. You're going to sacrifice us... to a giant polar bear?"

"That's right," smiled Doris.

"I think it's time we left," Dave said to the others. He turned towards the door, but when he did, he saw that there was a huge army of strays standing behind them. Somehow the icy skeletons had crept in without making a sound.

"Oh my," said Captain Nitwit, as he, Carl and Spidroth turned around too.

Dave put his hand on the hilt of his sword, ready to draw it.

"Once again, I am dreadfully sorry about this, my dears," said Doris. "It's nothing personal."

There was a twanging of bows and Dave felt a sharp pain in the leg. He looked down and saw an arrow sticking out of his calf. He looked over and saw that Carl, Spidroth and Captain Nitwit had been hit by arrows too. Dave tried to draw his sword, but he was moving so slowly.

"Those arrows are tipped with a slowness enchantment," said Doris. "Once again, I am sorry about all this. You must think I have no manners at all! But if it makes you feel any better, it will all be over soon."

CHAPTER SEVEN
The Cart

Dave and the others were dragged down the stairs out of the castle by the strays. There were so many of them that even if he had been able to move at normal speed, Dave wasn't sure that he would have been able to fight them all. The strays had tied his hands together with rope anyway, so there was no way he'd be able to use his sword.

Outside of the castle, the strays had hitched some sort of wooden cart to a polar bear. Dave, Carl, Spidroth and Captain Nitwit were thrown in the back of the cart, then the stray riding the polar bear yelled something in his strange language and the polar bear began moving, dragging the cart across the ice. The other strays walked alongside the cart, guarding it as it trundled along.

The strays didn't seem to realize that Carl's body was actually a golem, so had just tied his diamond hands together.

"Carl, do you think you can break those bonds?" Dave asked.

Carl nodded, and pulled his wrists apart, breaking the rope instantly. Next he grabbed the rope around Dave's wrists and broke it, then did the same for Spidroth and Captain Nitwit.

They hadn't taken their weapons, thankfully, so Dave, Spidroth and Captain Nitwit still had their swords. They had no more arrows though, having used them all on the polar bears.

"What's the plan?" Carl whispered. "We may be free, but we're still surrounded by hundreds of strays."

"We'll have to fight our way out," said Dave. "I don't think we've got much of a choice. I don't like the sound of that giant bear that Doris was talking about."

34

"As if those other bears weren't big enough," whimpered Captain Nitwit.

Dave peered over the side of the cart. Walking alongside them were hundreds of strays, all of them holding bows. How were they going to fight their way out of this one?

And then he had an idea.

"Ok," he whispered to the others, "here's the plan. We're going to burn the cart."

"Er, what?" said Carl.

"It's the only way," said Dave. We set fire to the cart, it melts the ice below us, we fall into the water and then we swim under the ice to make our escape."

"Fool," hissed Spidroth. "Don't you remember what happened to us the last time we swam under ice? We almost drowned and then we almost got killed by drowned. Have you forgotten what happened to Little Billy?!"

"I haven't forgotten anything," said Dave, "but I can't see what other option we have. If we try and fight the strays with our swords, they'll fill us full of arrows. And if we don't do anything, they're going to take us to be eaten by a giant bear. Our options are limited."

"I hate to admit it," sighed Carl, "but I think Dave might be right. I'll have to leave my golem suit behind, I guess. I can't swim with it."

"We'll find you another one," said Dave. "I promise. But what's important now is that we escape with our lives."

"I still think it is a foolish plan," said Spidroth.

"Do you have a better one?" asked Dave.

"Hmmph," said Spidroth.

"Anyone else got any other objections?" asked Dave.

No-one did.

"Right," he said, "here goes."

He reached into his rucksack and pulled out a flint and steel.

"Ok," Dave said to the others, "when the cart starts to burn, keep to the sides to avoid the flames. Hopefully the ice will melt pretty quickly, so we'll drop into the water before the fire becomes a problem. If it doesn't, get off the cart and wait on the ice. When the ice opens up, swim underwater and we'll try and find another opening to swim to. I'll take Carl with me, since he can't swim that well."

"And what if we can't find another opening in the ice?" asked Captain Nitwit.

"Then I'll use my pickaxe to make one," said Dave. "Just stay with me. Ok... is everyone ready?"

They all nodded.

"Ok," said Dave, getting ready to light his flint and steel, "let's do this."

He struck the flint and steel against the wood in the middle of the cart, and it burst into flame. Dave, Carl, Spidroth and Captain Nitwit all moved to the edges of the cart, getting as far away from the flames as they could.

Dave heard some of the strays start to mutter in their strange voices as they noticed the fire. The stray riding on the polar bear turned around and began shouting.

Come on, Dave thought, looking at the fire, *melt the ice! Melt the ice!*

But the ice wasn't melting. The fire spread to the edges of the cart, so Dave and his friends had to quickly jump off of it to avoid getting burnt.

The strays standing around the cart were looking on in confusion, wondering what to do. The flames burned through the ropes tying the polar bear to the cart, and the polar bear roared then ran off to escape the flames, trampling strays as it went. The poor stray on the back of the polar bear was clinging on for dear life.

Dave looked back at the cart. It was completely on fire now, so why wasn't the ice below it melting?

Then Dave looked down and realized what was going on. The ice the cart was standing on... was packed ice.

Dave quickly pulled out his pickaxe. They couldn't melt their way through the ice, but maybe they could dig a hole through it instead. He was about to swing his axe down when he felt bony fingers grab his wrist. The strays had finally moved into action, grabbing Dave and the others.

"Get off me!" Carl was yelling, swinging his golem arms and trying to get the strays off of his back. Captain Nitwit and Spidroth were trying to get free too, but the strays were holding them down.

"Get away!" Spidroth was yelling. "Don't you know who I am?!"

Dave tried to reach for his sword, but the strays were holding on to him tightly with their bony hands. Then a stray walked up to him and biffed him in the face, and everything went black.

CHAPTER EIGHT
The Ceremony

When Dave awoke he was being carried along by the strays, his hands tied up once more. They were carrying him up the slope of a huge iceberg mountain. Dave looked around and could see that they were far above the ocean now. They were so high up that they had almost reached the clouds, and Dave could see the endless expanse of ice and ocean stretching out far below them.

Nearby, Dave saw that the strays were carrying Captain Nitwit and Spidroth too, both of whom were unconscious.

Carl was being carried along by the strays as well. The little creeper was unconscious and had been removed from his diamond golem suit, but, weirdly, the strays were carrying the empty suit along as well.

"Hello, Dave," said a kindly voice.

Dave turned and saw Doris. She was sitting on her wooden throne, which the strays were carrying along on their backs.

"You," said Dave angrily. "How can you do this to us? You're really going to sacrifice us to a bear?"

"A giant bear," said Doris with a smile. "I call her the Giga Bear. I can't pronounce the name the strays use for her."

"So this is what you do whenever someone lands on the ice?" asked Dave. "You sacrifice them to the Giga Bear?"

"As I said, pet, it's nothing personal," smiled Doris. "It's for the strays really, it keeps them happy. They worship the bear, and sacrificing other people to them means that they don't sacrifice me."

Suddenly Dave was struck by a feeling of horror.

"Wait," he said, "the deal you made with the strays... you let them take your family, didn't you?"

Doris giggled.

"Ok, you've got me," she said. "I might have told a bit of a lie when I said I was the only survivor of the shipwreck. Most of my family and our crew survived too. It wasn't long before half of us were captured by the strays, me included. The rest went back and hid in our crashed ship.

"When I realized that we were going to be sacrificed, I made a deal with the strays: I showed them where the others were hiding, and in return they let me live."

"You sacrificed your own family," said Dave, appalled.

"Oh, trust me, it was no big loss," smiled Doris. "They weren't very nice people. Ooo, looks like we're here!"

The strays had come to a stop at the top of the iceberg mountain. The ice had been flattened up here, and there was something that looked like a stadium made of ice in front of them.

"Take them to the pit," Doris told the strays. "Give the creeper his armor back though, we want to give the bear a bit of a fight. Goodbye Dave," she added. "It really was nice to meet you."

Dave didn't give Doris the satisfaction of a response as the strays carried him and his friends towards the stadium.

"What's going on?" muttered Carl, as he began to wake up.

"We're in trouble again," said Dave.

"We're always in trouble," sighed Carl, looking around at the strays. "Hey, what are they doing with my golem suit?"

Spidroth and Captain Nitwit were starting to wake up too.

"What happened?" asked Captain Nitwit sleepily, "did we escape?"

"Yep, we've escaped," said Carl. "We're being carried along to the cake shop to get some lovely cake to celebrate."

"Ooo, I do love cake," said Captain Nitwit.

"Get off me fools!" Spidroth yelled, trying to pull free from the grip of the strays. But there were simply too many of them.

The strays carried them through a tall tunnel with ice walls that led into the building. Once they passed through the tunnel they emerged into the middle of a gigantic open-air stadium made completely of packed ice. On the seating stands around them were hundreds, maybe thousands, of strays, all cheering in their croaky voices. It reminded Dave of the stadium that the wither skeletons had brought him, Carl, Porkins, Robo-Steve and Alex to when they'd tried to sacrifice them to a wither, but much, much bigger.

I guess skeleton creatures just like to make sacrifices, Dave thought.

In the middle of the stadium was a huge pit that was so deep that Dave couldn't see the bottom of it. The seating stands had been built quite steep, so all the strays could get a good view of the pit.

The strays brought Dave and his friends to the side of the pit and dumped them on the ground. Then they cut the ropes around their wrists and dumped Carl's golem armor next to him.

"I guess they want us to be able to fight," said Carl, wriggling into his golem armor. "They may live to regret that."

Dave was still wearing his diamond armor, and he drew his diamond sword. He wanted to be ready for whatever happened next.

"Oh my," whimpered Captain Nitwit. "Oh my, oh my, oh my!"

The Captain was looking down into the pit. He looked terrified. Dave had a look down himself, and suddenly he was seized by fear as well.

The huge pit went deep into the iceberg, with walls that were vertical sheets of packed ice. But what terrified Dave wasn't the pit itself, it was what was at the bottom of the pit: a colossal polar bear with glowing red eyes. It was standing on two legs, looking up at Dave and the others with its sharp teeth bared.

"ROOOOOOOOOOOOOOOOOOOOAAAAAARRR!!!!!"

The polar bear's roar was so loud that it shook the iceberg, and Captain Nitwit almost fell down the pit.

"Help!" he yelled.

Dave grabbed the Captain just in time, pulling him away from the edge. The strays on the stands above them let out a loud cheer.

"How the heck are we meant to fight that thing?" said Carl, looking down at the bear. "It's massive!"

"Any foe can be defeated, no matter how large," said Spidroth. Although Dave could sense a bit of fear in her voice.

Dave had another look down at the bear. It really was huge, and it looked angry too.

I wonder what it eats? he thought. A bear that size surely had to eat a lot of food, not just the occasional sacrificed villager. But then Dave noticed that the floor of the pit was covered in half-eaten fish.

So that's why the strays catch all those fish, Dave realized. They weren't eating the fish themselves, they were feeding them to the Giga Bear.

There was another big cheer from the stands. Dave looked up and saw that the strays were carrying Doris through the crowd on her throne. Dave was annoyed to see that she still had a little sweet smile on her face.

The strays put Doris's throne down on a balcony overlooking the pit, and she began to speak into some sort of ice-horn device on the edge of the balcony, her voice amplified so that it echoed across the stadium.

"Hello, pets," said Doris. "I hope everyone is having a lovely day today."

"She really is a mad old bat," said Carl.

"She's not mad, she's evil," said Dave.

"We're gathered here today for the sacrificial ceremony," continued Doris. "I know it's been a while since we had one, but the gods have been lucky enough to bring us four lovely sacrifices for the Giga Bear. All hail the Giga Bear, the god of the ice."

The strays all chanted something in their icy language. Dave assumed they must be saying *All hail the Giga Bear*, or something similar.

"Now, it's been a while since the Giga Bear has been fed, so he must have a bit of an empty tummy," said Doris. "So let's not waste any more time—on with the sacrifice!"

The strays all cheered.

"Well, let's look on the bright side," said Carl, "that pit is so deep that we'll die from fall damage, so at least we won't be eaten alive."

"Prepare the Arrows of Slow Falling!" said Doris.

"Oh great," said Carl. "I just can't catch a break."

Four strays with bows stepped forward and pulled back their arrows, ready to fire at Dave, Carl, Spidroth and Captain Nitwit.

"Maybe we should just jump into the pit now," said Captain Nitwit. "A quick death has got to be better than falling slowly towards that bear."

Dave hated to admit it, but maybe the Captain was right. What else could they do?

"That poor beast," said Spidroth, looking down at the Giga Bear. "Such a magnificent creature should not be kept imprisoned like this. It should be free to roam the land, slaying anything in its path."

"That *magnificent creature* is going to be eating us in a minute," said Carl. "So don't feel too sorry for it."

But something about what Spidroth said had given Dave an idea. It wasn't a great idea, and it probably wouldn't work, but it was the only idea he had.

"Get ready to fire!" Doris yelled, her voice booming around the stadium.

The four strays all pulled back their arrows.

Here goes nothing, thought Dave. He reached into his bag and pulled out the remaining three bottles of strength potion he'd found in the submarine, then dropped them all into the pit.

The potions fell down, down, down, then *splish*, they cracked open against the Giga Bear's head.

"What are you doing?" said Carl, looking at Dave. "You're making the bear stronger, you idiot!"

"I hope so," said Dave.

Dave looked down the pit at the bear.

"Oi, bear!" he yelled. "What are you doing down there being all stupid? You're just a dumb bear!"

"You really are rubbish at insults," sighed Carl.

But it worked. The bear roared in frustration and began hitting the side of the pit with its paws.

The whole iceberg began to shake as the bear continued to pound the wall. Some of the strays on the stands went flying, falling down, down, down, into the pit, right into the bear's jaws.

"*ROOOOOOOOOOOOOOOAAAAAAAAARRRRR!!!!*" the bear yelled, smashing its huge paws into the ice wall once more. This time there was an audible *CRACK*, and iceberg mountain began to break.

The strays were all beginning to panic now. The four strays with the Arrows of Slow Falling had dropped their bows and were running as fast as they could away from the pit. The ice stadium itself was starting to crack too, and more and more strays were falling from the stands, screaming as they fell into the pit.

"What's going on?" Doris shouted, fear in her voice. "What's going on?!"

Half of the stadium collapsed and fell straight into the pit, shattering on top of the bear's head. But that just made her all the more mad, and she

41

pounded on the walls of her pit harder than ever.

"Come on," Dave said to the others. "Let's get off of this mountain before there's nothing left of it!"

They began to run towards the tunnel that led out of the stadium. The strays were so busy trying to escape that they didn't try to stop them.

"Wait!" Doris yelled, her voice echoing across the stadium through the ice pipe. "Don't leave me!"

Dave looked up and saw Doris looking down pleadingly from her balcony. The strays had abandoned her and she was all on her own.

"I'm going to save her," said Dave.

"Have you lost control of your brain?" shouted Carl. "She tried to sacrifice us to a giant bear!!"

"The creeper is right," said Spidroth. "She deserves everything that's coming to her."

"I have to agree with those two," said Captain Nitwit. "Come on, Dave, she doesn't deserve saving."

Dave looked up again at Doris. As evil as she was, she was still an old woman who needed help.

"You all get off the mountain," said Dave. "If we all survive, I'll meet you at the bottom."

"Well, if you're staying we'll stay with you," said Carl.

"No," said Dave. "You need to go. Now!"

Carl sighed.

"You're a nutter, you know that?" he said to Dave.

"Go!" shouted Dave.

So Carl, Spidroth and Captain Nitwit reluctantly ran off, leaving Dave on his own.

"Help me, Dave!" Doris shouted. "Help me!"

Dan ran up a set of icy stairs that went up the side of the stadium, pushing past the strays who were running the other way to escape. The stadium was almost empty now, so it didn't take him long to reach Doris's balcony.

"Thank you, dear!" she said when she saw Dave. "Ooo I was so scared!"

"Come on, get on my back," said Dave, leaning down next to the wooden throne. Doris reached over and put her arms around his shoulders, then Dave began to carry her.

"You are awfully strong, pet," said Doris, as Dave carried her down the stairs.

"Shut up," he said. "When all this is said and done I'm going to make sure you go to prison."

"That's fair, dear," said Doris. "I suppose I have killed a lot of people."

CHAPTER NINE
Escape

Dave ran down the side of the iceberg mountain as fast as he could—which wasn't very fast as he had to be careful not to slip on the ice and was still carrying Doris on his shoulders. Thankfully the old woman didn't weigh very much.

"Ooo, careful dear," she said, "it's very slippery. You don't want to do yourself a mischief."

Dave wasn't quite sure if Doris was evil, insane, or maybe a bit of both, but he was already regretting his decision to go back and save her. The whole mountain was cracking and breaking beneath their feet, and Dave thought that it wouldn't be long before it collapsed completely.

They were halfway to the bottom of the mountain when suddenly there was a mighty *KER-ACK!!!* behind them. Dave looked around at an explosion of ice behind them as the Giga Bear finally burst free from the mountain.

"*ROOOOOOOOOOOOOOAAAAAAAAARRRRR!!!*"

"Oh my," said Doris.

Dave ran faster down the mountain, blocks of ice raining down from the sky all around him. The mountain was collapsing, and he had to keep jumping out of the way as huge cracks appeared in the ice.

Then, just as he thought things couldn't get any worse, Dave heard the stomping of huge footsteps, and looked around to see the Giga Bear running down the mountain towards him and Doris.

"Ooo we are in a pickle!" said Doris.

Dave ran as fast as he could, but the Giga Bear was gaining fast, shaking the iceberg as it ran. But then the iceberg completely collapsed, an avalanche of ice blocks tumbling down the slope. Dave jumped onto a packed ice block and used it to surf the wave of falling blocks, trying his hardest to keep from falling off.

"ROOOOOAAAARRRR!!!!"

Dave turned and saw that the Giga Bear had lost its footing in the avalanche, and was tumbling down the slope behind them.

"Faster, Dave!" Doris shouted. "Come on, dear, faster!"

Dave bent his knees, trying to speed up. They were nearing the bottom of the iceberg now, and he was trying desperately to keep his balance on the ice block he was surfing on.

Dave and Doris reached the bottom of the mountain and went skidding across the ice, Doris falling off of Dave's back as they both tumbled across the ground.

"RRROOOOAR!!!"

The Giga Bear reached the foot of the mountain a second after they did, smashing the ice sheet below them to bits. The ice broke beneath Dave's feet and he plunged down into the cold water. He felt something stirring in the water below him, and looked down to see the Giga Bear swimming towards him, its jaws open, ready to swallow him whole.

Dave kicked his legs as hard as he could, reaching the surface of the water and then pulling himself up onto the ice sheet. Doris was sitting on the ice already.

"Are you alright, dear?" she asked.

Suddenly the Giga Bear burst from the water, landing on the ice sheet next to them. It snarled as it looked down on them, pure anger in its eyes. Dave drew his sword. Even though he knew he didn't stand a chance against the colossal bear, he wanted to go out fighting.

"Stay away, you beast!"

Dave turned and saw Spidroth, Carl and Captain Nitwit rush over to join him. Captain Nitwit was trembling like crazy as he looked up at the massive bear, but he was still holding a sword, ready to fight.

"We couldn't let you get eaten by a giant bear on your own," said Carl. "Good friends get eaten by giant bears together."

The bear growled, looking like she was going to attack at any moment.

"Well I must be off," said Doris, getting gingerly to her feet. "Good luck with the bear. It really was lovely to meet you!"

And then she ran off across the ice.

"She can really move when she wants to," said Carl.

"Ok then, beast," said Spidroth, gripping her sword and looking up at the Giga Bear. "Let's make this a battle that will go down in history."

Dave and his friends stood defiantly in front of the giant bear, ready to do battle. But then there came a sound from nearby:

"ROAR!"

Standing on the slopes of a nearby ice hill were hundreds of normal-sized polar bears, all looking up at the Giga Bear. Then, to Dave's amazement, the polar bears all lowered their front legs and dipped their heads.

"Are those bears... bowing?" asked Carl.

"I guess they see the Giga Bear as their god too," said Dave. "Maybe that's why they were so angry and aggressive—they were mad that the strays were keeping their god prisoner."

The Giga Bear lifted its head and let out a roar that was so loud that it hurt Dave's ears:

"ROOOOOOAAAARRRR!!!!!!!!!!!"

And then the Giga Bear ran off across the ice, smashing apart all the icebergs and ice hills in its way. The other bears all ran off after it, roaring happily.

"Look!" said Captain Nitwit, "it's running straight towards the castle!"

Nitwit was right. The Giga Bear ran straight into the strays' ice castle, shattering it to bits. The bear was so big that it didn't seem to feel the castle shattering down around it, and it just kept running. Soon the Giga Bear and the polar bears had all disappeared from sight

"Whew," said Captain Nitwit. "That was a lucky escape."

THUNK!

An arrow plunged into the ice, just missing Dave's feet.

"Oh great," said Carl. "The strays are back!"

Carl was right, Dave saw. Hundreds of strays were running towards them across the ice.

"Wait!" Dave shouted out them. "Don't hurt us! We saved your queen!"

"Um, I don't think they're listening, Dave," said Carl.

"In that case," said Dave, "run!!!"

CHAPTER TEN
Goodbye

Dave, Carl, Spidroth and Captain Nitwit ran as fast as they could, but the strays were gaining on them fast.

"Let me carry you all," Carl yelled. "I can run faster than you can in my golem suit."

"The Lady Spidroth will not be carried like a bag of potatoes!" snapped Spidroth.

"Until a couple of weeks ago you *were* a potato," said Carl. "So swallow your pride and let me carry you!"

Carl didn't wait for Spidroth to reply, he just picked her up and put her on his right shoulder. Then he picked Captain Nitwit up and put him on his left shoulder.

"What fun!" said Captain Nitwit.

"Pah!" said Spidroth.

Finally, Carl picked Dave up and held him in his arms like a baby.

"Ok, now let's get some proper speed going," said Carl. He ran as fast as the golem suit would take him, moving his diamond legs so fast that to Dave they just looked like a blur.

Before long they'd left the strays far behind.

"Good one, Carl!" said Dave.

But just when they thought they'd escaped, things suddenly got a lot worse. Up ahead in the distance they could finally see the end of the frozen ocean biome, and there was nothing but empty blue ocean beyond it.

Carl skidded to a stop at the edge of the ocean and put the others down. Dave heard the sound of bony footsteps, and looked round to see the strays still running towards them across the ice. They were trapped: with the ocean on one side and strays on the other.

The strays came to a stop just within arrow firing distance of Dave and his friends.

"Please listen to me," Dave said to the strays. "Speak to your queen. She'll clear all this up."

And then Doris walked out from between the strays.

"Hello, dears," she said with a smile. "How are you all doing?"

"Doris," said Dave, "thank goodness. Please tell your people to let us go."

"I'm afraid not," said Doris.

"What?" said Dave. He couldn't believe what he was hearing.

"I'm dreadfully sorry, dears, but I still can't let you escape," said Doris. "We may not have our lovely Giga Bear anymore, but my lads still want to see a sacrifice."

"I saved you!" said Dave in disbelief. "I saved your life!"

"And I am very grateful," smiled Doris. "Really I am."

The strays all pulled back the arrows on their bows, preparing to fire.

"Goodbye, pets," Doris said. "This really is nothing personal. FIRE!"

The strays fired their bows, but suddenly something huge and blue smashed through the ice in front of Dave, Carl, Spidroth and Captain Nitwit, landing in front of them.

Thunk, thunk, thunk, thunk, thunk! The arrows hit the creature, who barely seemed to feel them. But Dave and the others were saved.

And then, to his shock, Dave realized that the creature was a drowned. The biggest drowned he'd ever seen, with huge, hulking muscles. In fact, it looked a lot like...

"Big Billy!" gasped Carl.

"BURRRRR!!!!!" bellowed the drowned. Dave realized that Carl was right: it was Big Billy, and he'd transformed into a drowned, with turquoise skin and rotten brown clothes.

"I can't believe it!" said Captain Nitwit happily. "Little Billy!"

"Big Billy," Carl corrected him.

"Drowned Billy," said Spidroth.

"Maybe we should just call him 'Billy'," said Dave. "It might be easier."

"Kill it!" Doris shouted. "Kill that awful thing!"

But suddenly the ice underneath the strays was breaking, and hundreds of other drowned were reaching up through the water, pulling them under. The strays tried to fight back but they didn't stand a chance: the drowned were pulling them into the water before they could notch their bows.

"No!" Doris whimpered. "Save me! Please, Dave! Save me! I'm just an old woman, I didn't mean any harm, I didn't—"

But whatever Doris had been about to say was lost as the ice beneath her broke, and she was pulled underwater by the drowned, their moldy hands dragging her under.

Before long all the strays were gone, leaving nothing but arrows and broken ice. The drowned had all disappeared too, going back beneath the water.

"Wow, Billy," said Carl, "are you the king of the drowned now, or something?"

"BURR," said Billy.

"It's good to have you back, Billy," said Dave. "Now, let's all sort out getting a ship. We still need to cross the ocean."

"BURR," said Billy.

"You're... you're not coming with us, are you?" said Spidroth sadly.

"BURR," said Billy.

"You're going to live with the drowned?" asked Carl.

"BURR," said Billy.

"Well, we're gonna miss you big guy," said Captain Nitwit.

"Yeah, we really will," said Dave, smiling. "Thanks for everything, Billy."

"BURR," said Billy. And then he jumped back into the water... and was gone.

"Spidroth," said Carl, "are you crying?"

"Of course not, fool!" said Spidroth, turning her face away, "there's just some salt water in my eyes."

They made their way back across the ice, towards the area where they'd seen all the shipwrecks, but when they got there all the ice and the ships had been smashed to bits, leaving nothing but blocks of wood floating in the water.

"The Giga Bear must have gone through this way," said Dave sadly, looking at the path of destruction.

"So now what?" asked Carl.

"I think we don't have a choice," sighed Dave. "I think we're going to have to make ourselves some wooden rowboats."

"Rowboats to cross the ocean? That's not a great idea," said Captain Nitwit. "One big wave and we'd end up capsizing."

"Well, does anyone have a better idea?" asked Dave.

No-one did.

"Right then," said Dave, plonking a crafting table down on the ice. "Let's build some boats."

EPILOGUE

Dave and the others had been rowing their boats for two days when they eventually saw land. Dave and Carl were in one boat and Spidroth and Captain Nitwit were in another, with a lead connecting the two boats so that they didn't get separated. They'd been stopping occasionally to eat and rest, taking turns to sleep so that there was always someone keeping watch to make sure that the lead didn't break or to sound the alarm if they were attacked.

"Land!" Dave yelled happily. "I see land!"

Everyone was excited, but as they got closer they realized that the "land" was just a small gravel and sand island in the middle of the ocean. Still, it would be nice to rest on dry land for the night, so they brought their boats ashore, put them in a chest, then Dave built them a small house with beds.

Once the house was built, the four of them sat on the sandy beach and watched as the sun went down.

"I hope Little B will be alright with his new friends," said Carl sadly. "The big-little guy deserves to be happy."

"Billy will make a fine drowned," said Spidroth. "I'm sure he will feast on the flesh of many sailors in the years to come."

"Spidroth, why do you have to make everything so unpleasant?" sighed Dave.

"I might head to bed," Captain Nitwit yawned. "All that rowing is hard work."

He stood up.

"Do you not want to finish watching the sunset?" asked Dave.

51

"I've seen plenty of sunsets in my time," said Captain Nitwit, smiling. "I'd much rather get some kip."

So Captain Nitwit headed off to the wooden house, leaving Dave, Carl and Spidroth sitting on the beach.

"Do you reckon we'll ever reach land?" Carl asked. "I mean, we might just end up sailing forever. Or at least until we run out of food."

"I know we will," said Dave. "The eye of enders were right before, when they led us to the end portal under Diamond City. Somewhere to the west there's another end portal, and we're going to find it."

Suddenly there was a flash of blue light on the beach next to them, and a mysterious portal appeared out of thin air.

"Battle stations!" yelled Dave, jumping to his feet and pulling out his sword. Spidroth pulled out her own blade and Carl stood up and clenched his diamond fists, ready for a fight.

The portal looked very similar to a nether portal, but it was light blue and had no frame. A figure emerged from the blue portal liquid, stepping onto the beach in front of them. It was a pigman.

Porkins! thought Dave. But no, he realized—it wasn't Porkins. This pigman was far too fat to be Porkins, but Dave was still sure he recognized him. But from where?

"Hello chaps," said the pigman. And then Dave knew where he knew him from.

"You're Trotter!" said Dave in amazement. "Trotter the Rotter! But... you're dead?"

Trotter smiled sadly.

"I'm awfully sorry about this, chaps," he said. "But I don't have enough time to explain at the moment. Please forgive me."

Trotter lifted up one of his fists and Dave saw that the pigman was wearing some sort of metal glove. A blast of pink light shot out from the glove, hitting him, Carl and Spidroth. For a moment, Dave thought the blast hadn't done anything, but then he fell to the floor, unable to move or speak. He could see Carl and Spidroth out of the corner of his eye, and they were in the same situation.

Some more figures came out of the portal, and Dave was amazed to see that they were a mixture of villagers and pigmen. Not zombie pigmen, but normal pigmen.

The villagers and pigmen lifted Dave, Carl and Spidroth up and carried them towards the portal. Dave tried in vain to move, but his body was frozen solid.

They passed through the portal and found themselves inside some sort of cobblestone building. The walls were shaking and villagers and pigmen were aiming arrows out of the windows. It seemed like they were in the middle of some sort of battle.

"What's going on?" Dave heard Trotter yell, as he stepped back through the portal.

"It's begun, sir!" said one of the villagers. "The enemy have found us! They have TNT cannons!"

The building shook once more, and Dave could hear an explosion somewhere nearby.

"Evacuate the children and the old folk at once," said Trotter. "We'll try to keep the enemy back as long as we can. Who's leading their army?"

"It's... um... it's..." muttered the villager nervously.

"Darn it man, who is it?" barked Trotter. "Who did the Emperor send?"

"It's the General," said the villager, his voice trembling. "It's... General Porkins!!"

TO BE CONTINUED...

Made in the USA
Monee, IL
21 March 2022

93266808R00031